COLLEEN McCROC

TRAIN MAN

UNCLE KENNY

JULIA

MICHAEL MULLIGAN

KOMODO DRAGON

CONNOR McCROC

CIARA McCROC

SIOBHAN
BRANAGAN

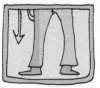

SEAMUS
BRANAGAN

SECURITY MAN

CROC MAN

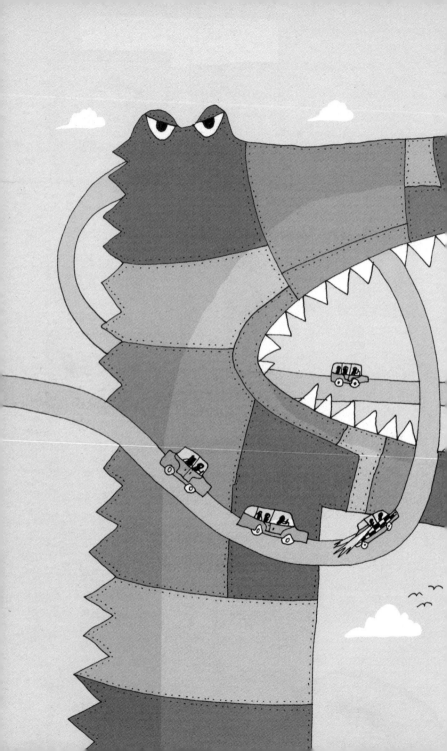

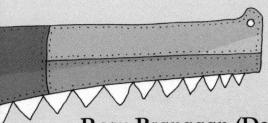

Rory Branagan (Detective)
The Leap of Death

by Andrew Clover
and Ralph Lazar

First published in Great Britain by
HarperCollins *Children's Books* in 2019
HarperCollins *Children's Books* is a division of HarperCollins*Publishers* Ltd,
HarperCollins Publishers
1 London Bridge Street
London SE1 9GF

The HarperCollins website address is
www.harpercollins.co.uk

3

ISBN 978-0-00-826595-3

Andrew Clover and Ralph Lazar assert the moral right to be identified as
the author and illustrator of the work respectively.
A CIP catalogue record for this title is available from the British Library.

Printed and bound in England by CPI Group (UK) Ltd, Croydon, CR0 4YY

MIX
Paper from
responsible sources
FSC **FSC™ C007454**
www.fsc.org

This book is produced from independently certified FSC™ paper
to ensure responsible forest management.

For more information visit: www.harpercollins.co.uk/green

Dedicated to all dads –
especially those who
read stories.

I am Rory Branagan, son of *Padder Branagan* – the *best dad of all time*.

When we went camping he would *tell stories*! The fire would be *crackling*, and the owls would be *hooting*, and the whole world felt *magic*.

When I was learning to *swim* I'd cling to his shoulders. He felt like a *warm, friendly island*.

And sometimes he'd THROW me in the sky, and I'd feel I was *flying* like a *jet*.

But, when I was three and a half, he *disappeared*. I felt I had crash-landed in a *swamp* filled with evil, squirming creatures, who all looked like my *brother*.

'Where do you *think* your dad is?' asks my friend Cat Callaghan one day when we're hanging out in the treehouse.

'Well, we know he was a World Rally *champion* . . .' I tell her.

'Yes, but he won't be *driving* rally cars now,' says Cat. 'You'd have heard about it if he was.'

'So I reckon he's in some far-off city,' I tell her, 'and he's DESIGNING them!'

'We also know he got mixed up with *criminals*,' Cat points out.

'So maybe he's *hiding* on some far-off *mountain*,' I suggest, 'only appearing when people need help.'

'But WHERE do you think that mountain IS?' says Cat. 'Do we have any *other CLUES* about where he's gone?'

I'm thinking: *Well, there is one MASSIVE clue that I haven't actually mentioned . . .*

A couple of months ago, my dad sent me a SECRET LETTER. In it he said he was hiding in the place he was once happiest.

He also told me not to tell *anyone* about the letter.

But the trouble is . . . ever since, questions have been *crammed* in my head like *cars* in a *car park*. I've been thinking: *But WHY can I tell no one?* . . . I think: *Does that mean MUM?* . . . I think: *But if I never tell ANYONE, how will I ever find DAD?*

So I tell Cat all about it now.

As I do she listens very carefully. Then . . .

'Don't worry, my little friend,' she says.
'I will find your dad for you!' Then she
pats me on the cheeks. *Pat, pat, pat.*

That does *slightly* annoy me.

'Well, *I* will probably be the one who
finds him,' I say, 'because *I* am the
detective!'

'Erm . . . It was actually *me* who fought the poisoners,' she says. 'It was ME who found the dog thieves.'

We *did* once fight poisoners. We *did* once find dog thieves. But . . .

'I AM A BETTER DETECTIVE THAN YOU!' I shout. 'You just get us into DANGER.'

'You're NOT a better detective,' says Cat. 'I mean . . . doesn't it *occur* to you that if your dad's *hiding*, he might have a *reason*? There are *bad people* out there, Rory. If you go looking for him, there *will be danger*!'

'I am not scared of that!' I say. 'If it helps me find my dad, I don't care HOW MANY BAD MEN I have to face!'

'Well, *don't* say I didn't warn you!' says

Cat.

And the very next day we find a clue that could lead us to Dad. BUT . . . we do definitely come up against DANGER. We come up against BAD PEOPLE. We also come up against ONE HUNDRED HUNDRED HUNGRY CROCODILES. I have to face my *VERY WORST FEARS!!!*

I'll tell you the whole story.

CHAPTER ONE:
A Blow on the Horn

It doesn't start, though, in deadly danger. As it *all starts* I am at home. Mrs Welkin is round, but she's outside in the garden with her dog, Wilkins. I am *alone*. I have just *allowed myself* the *luxury* of a fart.

And it's a good one. It has a warm, eggy smell. It's as loud as one from Wilkins, and that's saying something. When that dog LETS RIP they hear it in France.

In olden times a king would blow his horn to make his knights come to him, and it's like that now. I've blown my horn . . .

And Cat appears at my front door.

'I heard that,'
she says. 'Which
room were you
in?'

I say,
'Kitchen.'

'Take me to
your lounge,'
she says. 'I am ready to show you I'm a
better detective.'

And she is sooo cat-like. She comes into
my lounge. She blinks her big green eyes
once . . . then . . .

. . . *two seconds later*, there's a noise at the front door.

'That's your brother,' she whispers. 'He's brought home a girl!'

I am thinking: *It is very, very unlikely my stinky brother has brought home a GIRL. He's more likely to have brought home a GOBLIN.*

'She is tall and thin,' says Cat, 'and wearing Doc Marten boots with a hole in one sole.'

'*How* do you even know that?' I snarl.

'She has a long, *light* stride,' says Cat. 'And if you *listen carefully*, you'll hear the boots *squeaking*.'

I sneak to the kitchen, hoping to prove Cat wrong.

I see my brother standing in the kitchen with a weird look *smeared* over his BIG HEAD. He's looking *pleased* but *embarrassed*.

Peeking through the crack by the hinge of the door, we see the girl. She *is* tall, thin and wearing Doc Marten boots.

'Hello,' she says.
We go in.
'I'm Julia,' she says.
'What made the hole in your boot?' asks Cat.
'I trod on a pin,' she answers, looking surprised.

Turning, Cat mouths, '*I am a better detective than you!*' And she wriggles her bum, like a cat wiggling its tail.

I now look at Julia carefully.

And with my highly trained detective vision *I* notice *a leaflet* in Julia's bag. I catch sight of two very interesting words . . . *'Michael Mulligan'*.

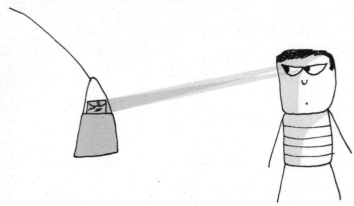

Michael Mulligan is a famous, dangerous *crime lord*. I came up against him when I was solving the Big Cash Robbery.

'Can I look at that?' I ask Julia.

She says, 'Sure!' She takes out the leaflet, and I cannot *believe* it, because it says . . .

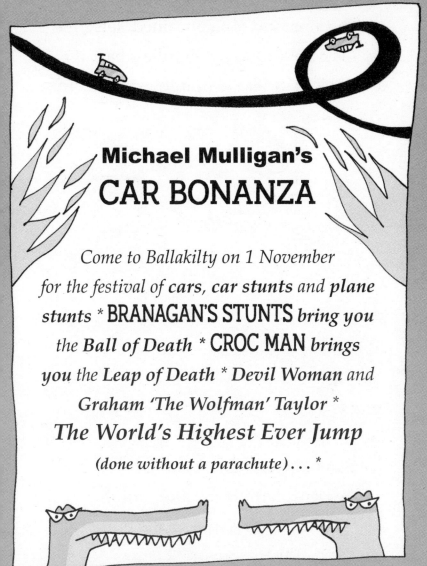

Michael Mulligan's
CAR BONANZA

*Come to Ballakilty on 1 November for the festival of **cars, car stunts** and **plane stunts*** * **BRANAGAN'S STUNTS** *bring you the **Ball of Death*** * **CROC MAN** *brings you the **Leap of Death*** * **Devil Woman** *and **Graham 'The Wolfman' Taylor*** * ***The World's Highest Ever Jump** (done without a parachute) . . . ***

The words 'Branagan's Stunts' *leap* out at me. I am thinking: *That could actually be Dad!* I lift the leaflet up to Cat's face.

'That is happening TODAY,' she says.
'Yes, and my dad could *be* there!'
'We should GO!' she says.
'We definitely should!' I agree.

But my brother never wants to go anywhere. (He just wants to stay all day lurking in the dark, being EVIL like a big fat slug.)

'There are LOADS of Branagans,' he says. 'And Ballakilty is *ten miles away*. If you tell Mum you've gone ten miles to go *detectiving*, she will throw you ten miles into *space*!'

'Well, *I'd* definitely like to go,' says
Julia. 'That's why I got the leaflet!'

'And *I* want to go,' says Cat.

'And I *definitely* want to go!' I say.

*'How are we all supposed to get to
Car Bonanza?'* shouts my brother (now
losing it).

Suddenly Mrs Welkin appears from the toilet.

'We could take the camper van,' she says.

I didn't even know Mrs Welkin was listening. It turns out she *was*, and she has a *camper van*.

We write a note for Mum and head out to see it.

CHAPTER TWO:
Camper Van

It is a huge thing that has *chairs* and *beds* and even a *kitchen*. It is BRILLIANT.

But it sure is slow!

As we set off towards Ballakilty we get
a *queue* of cars behind us.

'Mrs Welkin,' I say, 'I think we're
making a traffic jam!'

'Oh, I don't call that a traffic jam,' says
Mrs Welkin. 'I call it a PARADE . . . and if
we hurry, we won't enjoy the view.'

Just then, we drive over the brow of the hill. The sun is *beaming* through the clouds.

We see the sea *sparkling* in the distance,
the mountains *looming*, and in the valley
we see *Car Bonanza* with its *fires* and *cars*
and *planes* . . . It looks EPIC.

We park in a field and head towards the action. Right away we see a massive sign for Daredevil Motors, the garage Dad drove for. There's a picture of him.

I am excited just seeing his picture. I'm thinking: *I can't believe I could be about to see HIM!*

We pass a car that looks like it was designed by aliens.

We pass a car that looks like it was designed by eejits.

We pass the
World's Highest
Ever Jump
(done without a
parachute). It's
a plane that will
take the jumper ten
miles into the sky so
they can LEAP out
on to a MASSIVE
TRAMPOLINE.

I am so, so scared
of heights. Just
seeing that makes
me feel SICK.

We pass a
Daredevil Motors
stall. I get a badge
of Dad. Cat and
Wilkins get red
horns. My brother
gets a head-to-foot
complete devil
outfit with horns
and a tail.

Mrs Welkin gets interested in a train. There's a tiny conductor man.

'Would you like a ride on the train?' he asks.

Mrs Welkin would.

The train only goes about fifty metres. But Mrs Welkin LOVES it. As she sets off she cheers, *'Poop poop!'* and she waves her flask of tea at the sky.

We're beside a queue of people waiting
to show tickets to two men dressed as
devils. Wilkins is noticing something
WRONG with those men. They have tails.

He wants to BITE those tails. I have to
drag him away.

As Mrs Welkin joins us again, I notice a sign saying 'Daredevil Motors – the home of the Branagans'. *That's US*, we're thinking, so we don't care about tickets. We just walk right in.

And THAT is how we enter the *scene of the crime* – Mrs Welkin, Wilkins Welkin, me, Cat, Julia and my brother.

We're looking at a large, *deadly* stage. High up, to the left, a cool control tower pokes up into the sky. A car stands outside it at the top of a steep cliff with a *road leading straight down*. It ends in a ramp that goes over the back of the stage.

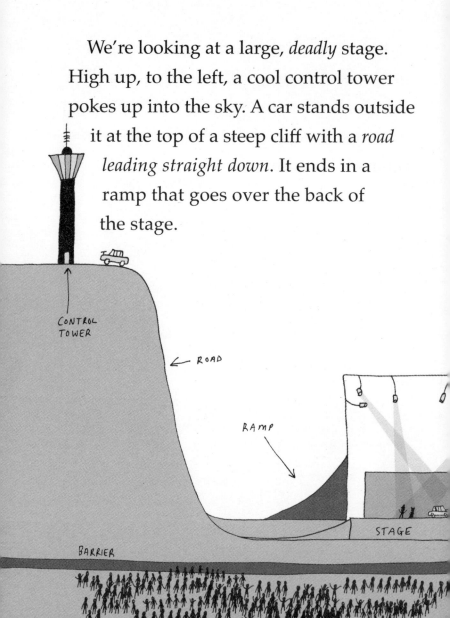

CONTROL TOWER

← ROAD

RAMP

STAGE

BARRIER

To the right there is the giant metal Ball of Death. A man (not Dad) is parking a car into position on the stage. It has cardboard flames at its side as if it's on fire. I'm sad I can't see Dad, but this does look good.

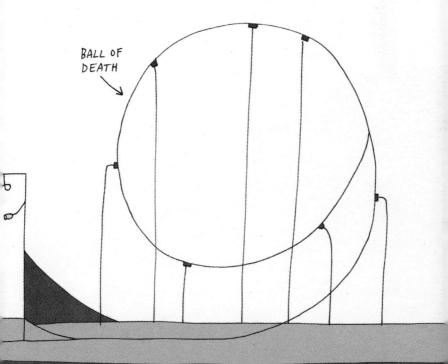

BALL OF DEATH

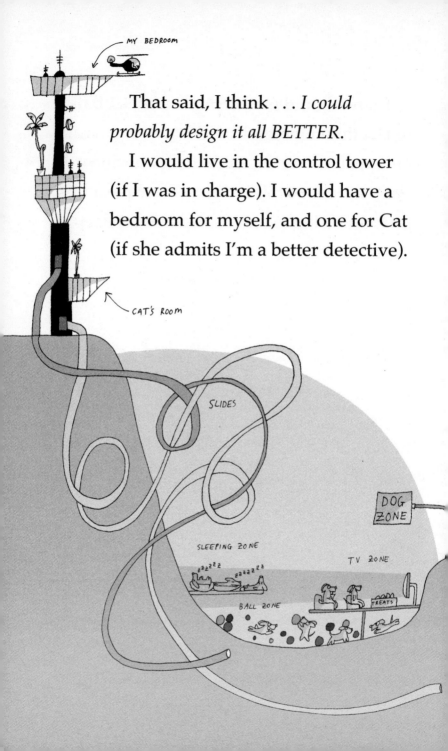

MY BEDROOM

That said, I think . . . *I could probably design it all BETTER.*

I would live in the control tower (if I was in charge). I would have a bedroom for myself, and one for Cat (if she admits I'm a better detective).

CAT'S ROOM

SLIDES

DOG ZONE

SLEEPING ZONE

TV ZONE

BALL ZONE

TREATS

Then I would have *slides* that would whizz down the cliff to the bottom, where I would have a *dog zone* for Wilkins and a *steam train* for Mrs Welkin, which would go round a big stinky *bog* (where I'd keep my brother).

My brother doesn't even look at any of this. He just sits down on a sofa and looks at Julia. She looks at him.

'I'll go and have one more ride on that train,' says Mrs Welkin. She gives me some money. 'Why don't you get yourself a drink?'

Cat and I get a Coke at a stall that has the Daredevil Motors picture. I tell the man that's my dad. He gives us another drink for free. We glug them right away. We are now feeling that the *whole world* is full of bubbles.

Wilkins is sniffing at a bean burger that someone dropped on the floor. He eats it down in three big gollops – gulp, gulp, gulp – then he does a fart that would knock Frenchmen from their bicycles.

Then Wilkins turns. He starts growling again. I look round and . . .

I notice one of the most *lethal*-looking women I've ever seen. Her back is to us and she has a full-on red-leather devil outfit.

The woman turns.

'It's Rory Branagan, the famous detective!' she says. 'I saw you on TV!'

I was actually on TV when I solved the Big Cash Robbery.

'I'm Kitty Malone,' she tells me. 'But most people call me Devil Woman.'

'Good to meet you, Devil Woman!' I say to her.

She smiles. She has blue eyes, a husky voice and *dimples*. (I think it is *impossible* not to like someone who has dimples!)

'And I am a GOOD FRIEND of your dad,' she says.

'WHAT?!!!' I say. 'Is he HERE?' And for a moment I feel so hopeful I could start rising like a bubble into the sky.

'Er . . . *no!*' she says. 'No one has seen *him* in seven years!'

Now I feel like the bubble's popped.

'But his SPIRIT is here!' says Devil Woman. 'Your dad invented half the stunts at this festival!'

'Did he?!' I say.

'It all started the first year he won the World Rally Championship,' she says. 'Your dad got his prize. He set up a stunt to celebrate. He zoomed off down a hill, went over a ramp and jumped over a hundred chickens . . .'

'The next year, he did the same – over one hundred pigs! That was the start of Car Bonanza!'

'The next year your dad did not win the rally,' says Devil Woman. 'He crashed. He *survived*, but, from that moment on, he didn't do any stunts. He sold the whole festival to Mulligan.'

I'm still *so* disappointed.

'I was sort of hoping Dad was here!' I admit.

'I'm sorry about that,' says Devil Woman,
'but your *uncle* is!'

'What?!' I gasp. 'Which one?'

'Your Uncle Kenny!' she says.

'*Uncle Kenny!*'

Uncle Kenny is my dad's younger
brother. I've not seen him in ages! I
remember once he swung me round and
round, then flung me two metres high into
a pool. He's a *NUTTER*!

He was also Dad's favourite brother! If anyone would know where Dad's gone, it'd be him!

'Where IS Uncle Kenny?' I ask.

'That's him right there,' says Devil Woman.

And she points to the driver in the cool car.

CHAPTER THREE:
Kid Kenny Branagan

There is a big barrier by the stage. But I don't care about that. I don't even tell Cat I'm going. I just leap right over the fence.

'*Uncle Kenny!*' I shout.

He turns. '*Jayzus, Mary and her husband Joe!*' he says. 'It's *Rory!*'

He leaps out of the car, he holds out his arms and we hug. He smells of petrol and leather . . . *He smells of Dad!*

'GET BACK!' calls a voice.

I turn to see a man with a massive Doberman. All *teeth* and *studs* and *muscles*, the dog strains towards me, wanting to BITE.

'That dog won't let anyone up who's not part of the show,' says Kenny. 'I'll walk you back.'

And he does.

'Rory!' says Kenny. 'It is SO good to see you! I don't think I've seen you since your dad went!'

'I know!' I say. 'Did Dad really design all these stunts?'

'*Man*,' he says, 'your dad *liked* rally driving. But stunts are what he LOVED. He *loved* it here!'

'Would you say this was where he was happiest?' I ask.

'Er . . . I suppose it might have been!'
says Kenny. 'Ah . . . I could tell you a
thing or two about your dad!'

I say, 'Do!'

'I've just got to break a world record
first!' says Kenny. He lifts up his arms.

'*Up, up and away!*' He walks back to the
car.

Suddenly there's an explosion.

People scream. Loud music sounds. The show is starting.

Up on the hill there's the deep rumbling of an engine.

Voom voom!

A massive bike reaches the edge of the cliff. A big man is on it. I can only see his silhouette but I know who it is.

VOOM!

'Hello, Car Bonanza,' says Michael Mulligan, and massive lights *beam* down to the stage. 'It is my privilege to present to you the *sickest* hosts of all!'

'A legend among stuntmen, *Graham "The Wolfman" Taylor* . . .'

A tall, stubbly man strides out on to the stage. The crowd roar.

'And the queen of Daredevil Motors, the Devil Woman herself, *Ms Kitty Malone*!'

Devil Woman leaps up too.

'Hello, Car Bonanza!' she says. 'You ready to have a good time?'

The crowd roar again.

'In one hour,' says Wolfman, 'Croc Man will perform the *Leap of Death . . .*'

'They have put a stunt car,' says Devil Woman, 'on top of that cliff.'

Where Michael Mulligan was just now, a car drives *over the edge of the cliff*.

People scream.

The car is almost vertical. *How does it not fall?*

'And inside that car . . .' says Wolfman, 'is *Croc Man*.'

Now the car door opens! A man slithers out of it.

He is half man, half *crocodile*. He has green skin. He has *fangs*.

'Croc Man will drive down that cliff,' says Devil Woman, 'going from nought to sixty in 1.6 seconds . . .'

'He will hit ninety as he drives down that road . . .' says Wolfman.

'He will HIT that ramp!'

'And he will FLY over . . .'

Devil Woman and Wolfman pull a covering from the back of the stage, revealing . . .

'ONE HUNDRED HUNGRY CROCODILES!'

I can't believe it. In the tank crocodiles are standing on the shoulders of crocodiles and you can tell each one is thinking . . .

I will eat that fat one.

I'm thinking: *It is horrible that someone is about to do this . . . but I definitely want to WATCH.*

CHAPTER FOUR:
The Ball of Death

'But who wants to see A WORLD
RECORD *now*?' says Wolfman.

EVERYONE roars.

'Who wants to meet the most famous
name in cars?'

'Ladies and gentlemen, we give you . . .'
Spotlights zoom down the stage.
'Kid Kenny Branagan!'
Uncle Kenny waves from his car.

'Kid Kenny will drive up the cliff,' says Wolfman. 'He'll turn. He will drive back this way, hitting a hundred miles an hour. Then he will drive into . . .'

'The twenty-metre-high BALL OF DEATH!'

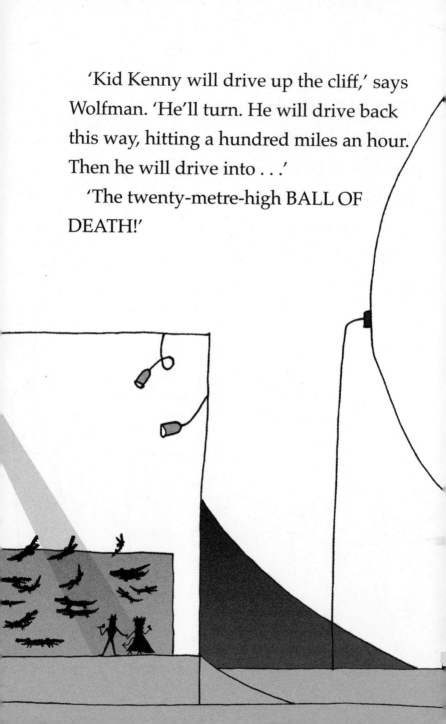

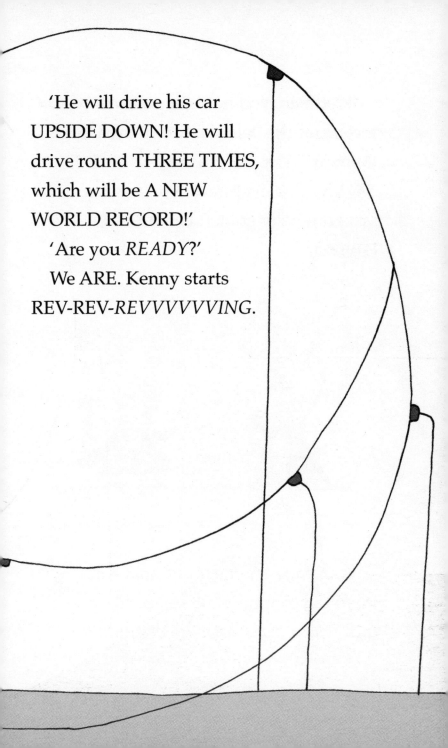

'He will drive his car
UPSIDE DOWN! He will
drive round THREE TIMES,
which will be A NEW
WORLD RECORD!'
     'Are you *READY*?'
     We ARE. Kenny starts
REV-REV-*REVVVVVVING*.

'Wolfman, you hold the current world record for the Ball of Death,' says Devil Woman. 'Why will this be so hard?'

'Have you ever swung on a swing so fast your belly got left behind?' says Wolfman.

'Yes!'

'As Kenny zooms round that ball,' Wolfman continues, 'it will be like that – *but a thousand times WORSE!*

'He'll be feeling SICK, he'll feel like his face is *falling off*, he'll be *blacking* out. It will feel like SHEER HELL!'

'BUT SHEER HELL,' says Devil Woman, '*is what we LIVE FOR each day at Daredevil Motors!!!*'

With that Kenny REVS one more
time, then leaves the flames behind and
CHARGES *straight up the road of death.*

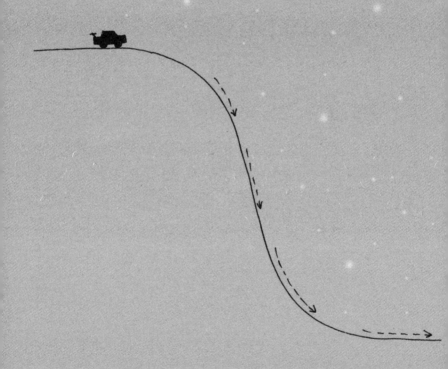

He climbs up towards Croc Man.
But then Kenny *turns*. He comes
speeding back down . . . then he SHOOTS
into the Ball of Death.

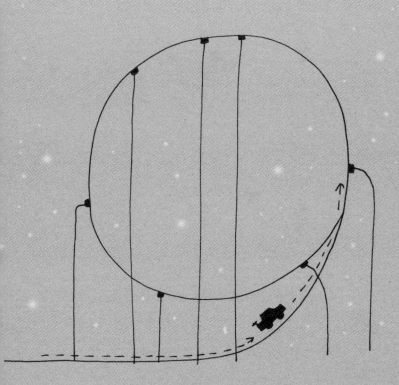

And then he is zooming UP the side.

Oh my God, the Ball of Death is *so* high.
Will he make it?

One moment he's upside down . . .

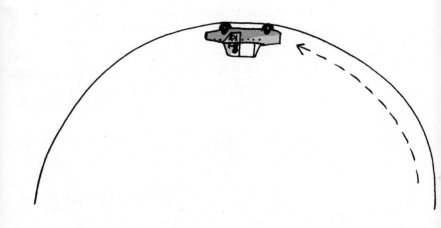

. . . then he's *shooting* round the side
again.

'*ONE!*' shouts Devil Woman.

But, as Kenny shoots down, his car seems to *cough*.

If you're trying to get round the Ball of Death three times, I am thinking, *your car should not cough!*

I also think the car's going *slower*.

But Kenny SHOOTS UP the side of the Ball of Death again.

He hits the top.

'*TWO!*' roar the crowd.

But, as Kenny shoots back down the other side, his car *coughs* again.

It also goes *rattle-rattle-rattle*. I am *certain* now that something's wrong. I am *certain* Kenny's slowing. I am thinking: *You won't make it the third time. STOP,* STOP, *PLEASE* STOP!

But us Branagans are DETERMINED!
Kenny wouldn't care if he had to go
UPSIDE DOWN round the **whole wide
WORLD**!

He keeps going up, up, up.
But his engine keeps coughing, and he's
DEFINITELY

SLOWING

DOWN!

Then for a tiny, tiny second, at the top of the Ball, he does STOP. And I'm thinking: *Is this part of the stunt? Can you stick cars to the ceiling?*

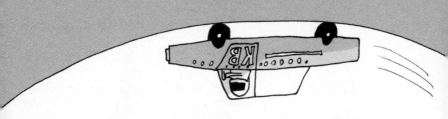

But of course you can't!

To my horror, the car starts to FALL.

I can't bear it. I shut my eyes as the car
falls like a *brick* . . .

KERRRRRRRRRASSSSSSSSSHHHHH

Around me the whole crowd gasps.

H!

Then there's silence. I open my eyes. I see Kenny's car upside down like a beetle on its back.

I see Kenny won't be telling me about Dad.

I see Kenny won't be telling me anything.

CHAPTER FIVE:
A Crime

I open my eyes. I am looking at Cat. Her face is so close I can smell her breath, which always smells a bit like Marmite and a bit like milk.

'You OK?' she asks.

I must have fainted. I stand up.

I see a big motorbike zooming across the stage. It's Michael Mulligan. He is followed by an ambulance. It skids over. Two people jump out with a stretcher.

A police car skids over even faster. A HUGE FIGURE comes out and heads like a rocket into the Ball of Death.

Is it a *rhino* powered by a *jet engine*? No, it's . . .

Stephen Maysmith, Police Detective!

'Oh no!' says Cat. 'Stephen Maysmith is here! Let's get in quick and *investigate*, before he closes up the whole area and arrests the wrong person.'

She leaps over the barrier. I follow. Wilkins follows too.

Inside the Ball of Death the ambulance men are yanking open the car. They are pulling Uncle Kenny out! He's *moving*! I can't believe it! He's *alive*!

They are lifting him on to the stretcher.

I am right there as they come out of the Ball of Death.

'*Uncle Kenny!*' I say.

He looks up at me. He's mumbling.

'Wait!' I shout to the stretcher men.

'What is he saying?'

I lean down.

'*Ar ring dong wid de anjen,*' he says.

WHAT? What does that mean?

'Give the man some air!' barks Stephen Maysmith. 'The important thing is he gets MEDICAL ATTENTION.'

'The important thing is he's alive,' says Michael Mulligan. 'Wolfman! Announce it . . . The show must go on!'

'Ladies and gentlemen,' says Wolfman, 'I have just spoken to Kenny Branagan. "The show must go on!" – that's what he said!'

He did not say that, I am thinking. He said, '*Ar ring dong wid de anjen.*'
But WHAT does that mean?

'People,' continues Wolfman, 'get yourselves some food! Get yourselves a drink. In one hour the Leap of Death will take place. Before then Croc Man has invited you to join him – *in his own private swamp!*'

I look around at the crowd.

It is one of those times when I really HATE grown-ups. *Uncle Kenny has just nearly died. They don't care! They are queuing for drinks. They are herding like pigs round the burger vans.*

'Ar ring dong wid de anjen'??!!!
It doesn't make any sense!
I feel I'm *sinking* into *confusion* like a *car*
in a *swamp*.

I say it again out loud . . .
'Ar ring dong wid de anjen!!'
What does it mean?

And then suddenly the answer comes zooming into my head.

'There was something **wrong** with the engine!' I tell Cat.

'I *know!*' she says. 'Did you *hear* it?'

'Do you they think they sent out the car with something *wrong* with it?'

'Unlikely!' says Cat. 'There would be a *bunch* of mechanics who'd have checked *everything*. If someone messed with the engine, I'd guess they did it *there!*'

She runs to the place Kenny's car was standing. She looks at the cardboard flames that were beside it.

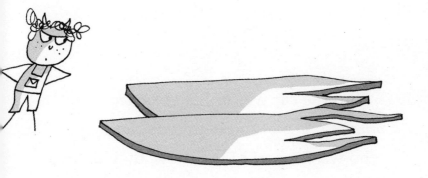

'These were hiding the petrol tank,' she says. 'Someone *could* have messed with the tank and not been seen!'

I HATE this.

I also HATE how she's solving this crime before I do.

'But the car was only here a *few minutes*,' I say, 'and if anyone came up who wasn't part of the show, they'd have been *GOT* by that Doberman!'

'Good *point*!' says Cat. 'So our suspects must all be people who *were part of the show*!'

So right away I'm seeing all possible suspects in my head.

Michael Mulligan (criminal)

Wolfman (shifty)

Croc Man (definitely weird)

The Man with the Dog (scary)

Devil Woman (dimples)

Could it be someone else?

'*Ah!*' says Cat.

'*What?*'

She is now on her hands and knees. Wilkins is beside her, poking his giant nose down a hole in the stage.

He shoots down it. Cat goes after him.

I realise they're about to solve this crime before me! I dive right after them.

CHAPTER SIX:
In the Dark

'Ah,' Cat says. 'LOOK!'

On her knees on the mud under the stage she shines her phone torch on something long and shiny.

It's a snake!

It's not a snake. It's a pipe. She picks it up carefully.

'*That's* how they drained the petrol out of the engine!' she says.

'*Ah*,' she says.

'What?'

She's found a plastic bottle of bleach.

'Here,' she says. 'Sniff that.'
'I am *not* sniffing that!' I tell her.

Wilkins takes the whole business of sniffing very seriously. He puts his giant nose to the bottle.

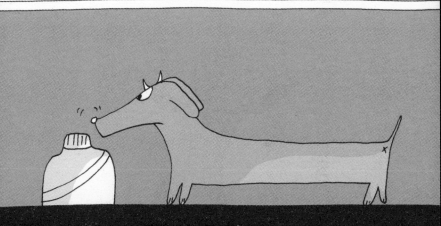

He sniffs it most professionally.

Then he looks up. And that dog is a detective. I just *know* he is working something out. What *is* it?

He's looking round to the back of the stage. You can see the croc tank. You can see a few of them writhing around in the darkness.

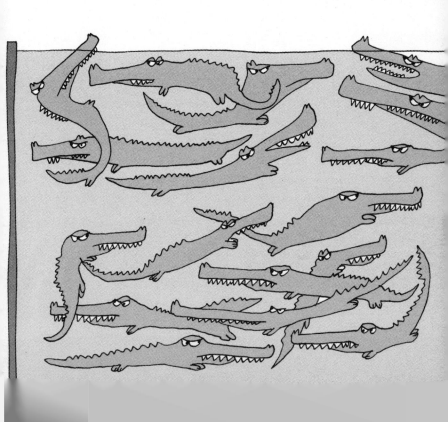

You can also see some legs. He *shoots* towards them.

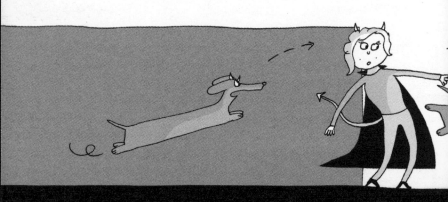

He comes tearing out of the back of the stage, almost banging into Devil Woman.

Wilkins doesn't know *what* the crime is or *who* Devil Woman is. He knows she has a tail. He *leaps* for it.

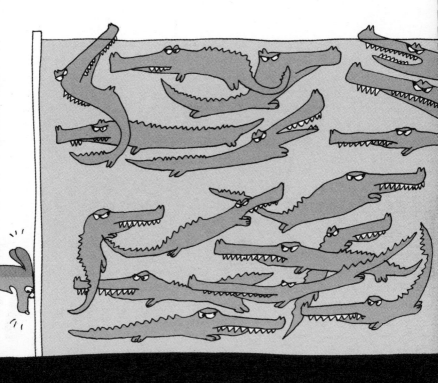

But she steps aside. I come out from under the stage to find Wilkins clonking into the crocodile tank. BONK.

Devil Woman is pleased to see me.

'*Rory Branagan!*' she says. 'Thank God you're here! Are you OK?'

'There was something wrong with the engine!' I tell her.

'What?!'

'Someone took the petrol out with a pipe,' says Cat. 'Then they filled it with bleach!'

'We think it happened just before the show,' I tell her, 'when you and I were talking.'

'Look,' she says, 'if someone messed with that engine, we need to tell the police!'

'I know if I go *near* Stephen Maysmith, he'll probably arrest *us*,' I tell her.

'We don't speak to the police,' says Cat.

'We prefer to solve the crimes *ourselves*,' I say.

'Well, I'll speak to them while you two find whatever you can!' she says, turning to go. 'We owe it to Kenny!'

'But wait,' I say. 'Try to *think* . . . Who might have wanted him dead?'

Devil Woman thinks for a second.

'*No one!*' she says. 'He was a *Branagan*! This whole show is based on the Branagans! Without a *Branagan* we'd lose everything!'

She hurries off.

'But maybe there was someone,' says Cat, 'who was about to lose something – *because of* a Branagan!'

'What do you mean?' I say.

'Well, there's Graham "the Wolfman" Taylor . . .'

'. . . Who was about to *lose his world record*!' I finish.

Just then, we both see the Wolfman. He's a tall man, and as he walks off towards his caravan he has a shifty *wolf-like* look on his face.

Right away I go cold.

CHAPTER SEVEN:
Graham 'The Wolfman' Taylor

We dodge behind a caravan.

'Why don't you get him talking?' says Cat. 'I'll search his caravan.'

'But what will I say?' I ask.

'You're Rory Branagan,' says Cat. 'You'll think of something!'

'*I don't think I will!*' I tell her. (She does this. She forces me into plans before I'm ready!)

'It doesn't matter *what you say*! Just say something!' And then she dumps me right in it. 'WOLFMAN!' she yells.

She pushes me out.

Wolfman turns. He sees me.

I see him.

'Yes?' he says.

'Graham "The Wolfman" Taylor?' I say to him.

'Yes?'

'Is that your real name?!'

'No!' he snarls. '*It's a nickname!*'

'But,' I say, 'if you have a cool nickname – e.g. *the Wolfman* – why would you keep your real name, if it's Graham?'

There's a silence, while the Wolfman seems to be thinking about biting my neck.

'Are you taking the mick?' he asks.

'*No*,' I say.

He turns to go.

'Kenny Branagan is my uncle,' I tell him. And suddenly my voice goes squeaky, and I realise I am about to cry. 'I think someone put bleach in his engine!'

He looks at me in terror. 'Then someone *did* try to kill him!'

Behind him I can see Cat. She and
Wilkins scuttle silently into his caravan.

I am terrified the Wolfman's about
to turn.

'Oh my God!' he whimpers. 'It could
be ME next!'

And he runs off in the other direction.
I now move quickly to his caravan.

I go in. I see – to one side – a small kitchen.

And – to the other – I see a bedroom.

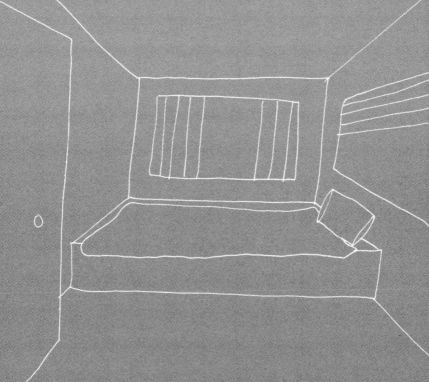

But I *can't* see Cat and Wilkins. My
heart goes BONG in my chest. I think:
What HAPPENED to them?

Then suddenly they LEAP out of the wardrobe!

'*Surprise!*' says Cat.

I nearly BELT her. '*Why did you do that?*'

'We heard someone coming so we hid,' she says, 'till we knew we were safe!'

'Did you find any EVIDENCE?' I ask her.

'Well, there's that,' she says, and she points at the wall of the bedroom, where there is a giant poster of Uncle Kenny.

It's been TORN and someone has written in black pen: *'I HATE KENNY BRANAGAN!'*

'I'd say that makes it *obvious* Wolfman *did* it!' I say.

'A touch *too* obvious – don't you think?' says Cat.

'What do you mean?'

'If you are about to *kill* someone,' she says (quite *patronisingly*), 'you don't put up a big poster of them where you say you HATE them!'

'It would be like Superman doing the crime,' says Cat, 'then leaving behind his pants!'

'WHY would Superman leave behind his pants?' I say (quite loud).

'I don't know!' says Cat. 'Maybe if he wet them?'

'Why would Superman have wet his pants?'

'Maybe if Lois Lane just said something really *funny*,' suggests Cat, 'and he LAUGHED SO HARD he wet his pants!'

'STOP TALKING ABOUT SUPERMAN'S PANTS!' I shout. (She is being SO unprofessional!)

I now approach the poster and I move my hand as if I were writing 'I hate Kenny Branagan' and that's when I notice something . . .

'Wolfman is tall,' I say, 'and people generally write at eye level. So he would write HIGHER than this!'

Then someone COMES IN. My heart beats.

Luckily it's just Devil Woman.

'I heard you two shouting in here,' says Devil Woman. 'What are you guys doing?'

'*Investigating*,' I tell her.

I point to the poster.

Her eyes flash. '*Scumbag!*' she says.
'So it's *obvious*: the *Wolfman* tried to kill
Kenny!'

'We think it's *too* obvious!' I tell her. 'It
would be like Superman leaving behind
his pants.'

She says, 'What?'

I can't believe I just said that! *(Cat's got
ME being unprofessional now!)*

'Let's get out of here,' I say, and I lead us out.

CHAPTER EIGHT:
The Croc Man

I am embarrassed I was just talking about pants. I am now *trying* to FOCUS on the crime.

'Whoever did this reached Kenny's car from under the stage,' I say, picturing it. 'They were *quick*. They were *silent*. They were also EVIL. They tried to frame the Wolfman so he'd take the blame.'

'So WHO did it?' asks Devil Woman.

I *think*, but I have no idea how this all fits together. I feel I am *sinking* into a swamp of confusion.

I have vague ideas, but they're like *shadowy shapes* hidden in the dark . . .

. . . And then I work it out.

'Can we speak to Croc Man?' I ask.

'Anyone can!' she answers. 'Before his stunt he's promised to speak to the public from his swamp. I'll take you up!'

'Did my uncle like Croc Man?' I ask as we walk.

'No,' she says. 'I couldn't say he did.'

'Why not?'

'In a festival like this everyone tries to be one big family,' says Devil Woman, 'but the truth is . . . they're all *competing* to be the one who gets the crowds, the attention, the TV interviews . . .'

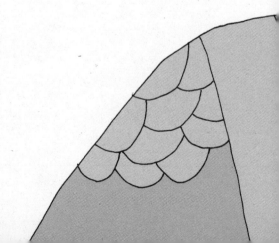

'And who gets the most attention?'

'Well, Croc Man has made himself look like a crocodile. That's freaky, and he is *very* popular.'

'But Kenny,' continues Devil Woman, 'is the brother of Padder Branagan. Just the name *Branagan* excites people.'

By now we're walking out into the crowds.

'Look at me,' she says. 'I'm dressed like a devil, and I was just onstage talking to the whole entire festival . . . but is anyone looking at me now?'

I look round at the people we pass. 'No,' I tell her. 'They're *not!*'

But then I see someone who is looking in our direction. *It's my mum!*

I didn't even know she was here. But now she is, she's about to find I've been *searching around, being a detective*. I'll be sent straight home and never allowed out again. *I'll never find who tried to kill Kenny*!

'Come,' I say to Devil Woman. 'I can see a quicker way up this hill!'

And I *dive* into the bushes. We're now going up through a very steep wood, but I don't mind. Wilkins and I *power* right up.

We come out on to a road.

We are on the hill that looks over the festival. I can see Michael Mulligan's tower pointing into the sky.

I can see the top of the Leap of Death and a crowd of people all waiting to see Croc Man. We can see the stunt car, waiting to drive off. We can see the fires and lights of the festival in the background. But we can't see Croc Man himself.

So we all gasp as he rises from the inky water.

'Before a stunt I like to keep cool,' he says.

He smiles a slow evil grin and a
thousand cameras flash.
'Any questions?' he says.
Loads of hands go up.
'Yes, sir?'

'Don't you think it's CRUEL?' someone says. 'You could be endangering the lives of those crocodiles?'

'I don't intend to hit them,' says Croc Man. 'And if I do, they won't be complaining. They'll be DINING!'

His eyes flash. *Oh my God*, I am thinking. *This man is CREEPY. He could definitely have tried to kill Kenny.*

'Another question?' he says.

Now hundreds of hands are up.

I know I'll never get picked. So I just *scream* from the back:

'DID YOU DRAIN THE PETROL OUT OF KENNY BRANAGAN'S CAR?'

Croc Man turns his head slowly.

'I couldn't have,' he says. 'I was up here, watched by a large crowd, and a million online followers.'

I am *so* angry with him.

'IS THAT ALL YOU WANT TO SAY,' I ask, 'WHEN KENNY BRANAGAN NEARLY DIED???!!'

Croc Man's yellow eyes turn oh so slowly. They look right at me.

'Maybe Kenny arranged it to happen *himself*. Look on YouTube . . . if a stunt goes well, twenty thousand people watch . . . If it *fails*, you get two *million* . . . Kenny just made himself *famous*. He made the whole *festival* famous. Next time Car Bonanza is on, *millions* will be buying tickets.'

I am thinking it is very *unlikely* Kenny ruined his *own* car.

But I also see Croc Man couldn't have done this.

Then I think of the person who will be making the money next year, if millions are queuing up for Car Bonanza.

And then I think of Michael Mulligan
lurking under us, like the biggest
crocodile of them all.

CHAPTER NINE:
Michael Mulligan

'Cat,' I say, 'we need to speak to Michael Mulligan.'

Something happens I've never seen before. Cat looks scared.

'Rory,' she says, 'I won't do that.'

'I've met him!' I tell her. 'He's not *that* bad.'

'So have I,' says Cat. 'And he *is*. I won't come!'

'So do you admit it then?' I say.

'What?'

'I am a better detective than you!'

'That won't be much good,' she says, 'if Michael Mulligan *crushes* you.'

'He couldn't *crush* me!' I say.

'He could crush you like you're ROADKILL!'

And I picture that, and I'm still not scared.

'I don't care how *big* or how *vicious* Michael Mulligan is!' I tell Cat. 'If he did something to Kenny, I'm going to *find out*!'

As I turn the sun is sinking and the sky is blood red behind Michael Mulligan's tower. Bats flap around it. I can actually see Michael Mulligan alone in there. His massive face is lit with the glow of his screens.

But I'm not scared.

I walk towards his tower. The path is lit up by lanterns in the shape of skulls.

That doesn't bother me at all.

On his big metal front door there's a
brass plate that says:

Michael Mulligan

Festival Director

Come in

(if you want to be shot)

That's just *pathetic*. The door clicks
open.

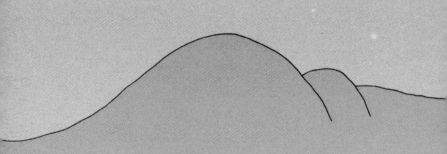

'Rory Branagan,'
rumbles Michael
Mulligan from upstairs.
'Come in!'
 I step right in.

A dragon LUNGES at my head.

It's Mulligan's Komodo dragon. He opens his massive mouth with its venom-tipped teeth.

I die ten deaths, but I see the dragon is on a chain. I edge round him.

I go up the spiral stairs, and I come out in Michael Mulligan's room. He has his back to me, but as I approach he turns. He looks at me.

Now I'm scared.

'Rory Branagan,' he says. 'What do you want?'

I gulp.

'Just before his stunt,' I say, 'someone took the petrol out of Kenny's car, then filled it with bleach.'

'And if I find out WHO,' Mulligan says, 'I will feed them to the DRAGON.'

I am scared to say more, but I know I must.

I say, 'Croc Man reckons because of Kenny's accident Car Bonanza will be even bigger next year.'

Michael Mulligan edges slightly forward.

'Are you *suggesting*,' he says, 'I might try *killing my stuntmen* in order to sell more tickets?'

I think: *That IS what I'm suggesting.*

I swallow. 'Where were you before the stunt?' I say.

'Up here on my bike,' he says. 'Watched by people, filmed by cameras . . . Where were you?'

'I was talking to Devil Woman,' I say.

'*Devil Woman?*'

'She's been helping us,' I say. 'She was a good friend of my dad's!'

'Oh, I wouldn't say *that*,' says Mulligan.

I'm surprised to hear that. 'But we
know *she* didn't do it!' I start to say. But
now *evil* thoughts are slithering into my
head.

I'm thinking: *Devil Woman IS part of the show.*

She COULD have started draining the petrol . . .

. . . then walked away . . .

That's why she was so friendly. She wanted an ALIBI to PROVE she wasn't under the car . . .

And I didn't see where she went when I was with Kenny. Maybe she RETURNED to the car and filled it with bleach . . .

Wilkins knew it from the first – he sniffed that bottle and led us straight to her. The Devil DID it!

'Where is Devil Woman now?' asks Mulligan.

'She was watching Croc Man with us.'

'We should find her,' he says.

'We definitely should!'

I turn for the door. But Michael Mulligan stops me with a question.

'Rory Branagan,' he says, 'where is your dad?'

Why is he asking me this?

'I don't know,' I tell him.

'Where would you say he was happiest?' says Mulligan, and his eyes beam into mine like headlamps.

I'm thinking: *Does he know about the letter?*

'Why do you want to know?' I ask.

'Your dad was a friend of mine,' he says.

So of course I am very keen to find out more about how Michael Mulligan knew my dad.

But right now I need to find Devil Woman. I know she's out there somewhere. *We need to GET her QUICK!*

I hurry out.

I open the door and look out at the night. I can see the crowds drifting away from Croc Man's swamp.

'Devil Woman!' I shout.

I see Mulligan's men – Guy 'The Eyes' Murphy and Derek 'Dent-head' O'Malley.

I see Cat and Wilkins.
I don't see Devil Woman.

But then I do.
She's close to Cat, and she's very *still*.
I see she's trying *suspiciously* not to be.

CHAPTER TEN:
The Leap of Death

On the balcony behind me Mulligan appears.

'Eyes, Dent-head!' he calls. 'Bring me Malone!'

They are looking around, but you can tell they can't SEE her.

And she is already quietly moving
away from them. She's getting close to Cat
and Wilkins.

'Cat, Wilkins!' I call. *'Get Devil Woman!'*

Devil Woman runs. She's *guilty* all right!

Cat shoots after her like a bullet.

Wilkins knows too. He's known she was guilty from the first. He also knows she has a tail. He soars after her like a furry *missile*.

He gets that tail in his teeth. He trips her up.

She stumbles. But she doesn't fall. She keeps running. I see she's going to the Leap of Death stunt car.

She reaches it. But Wilkins has slowed her down. As Devil Woman grabs open the front door . . .

. . . Cat reaches the other one.

She jumps in.

The door is still open. Wilkins LOVES cars. He thinks he's being invited on a walk. He jumps in too.

So now Devil Woman is in, Cat's in and so's Wilkins . . . *What should I do?*

I jump in too.

I land on Cat's lap. *Voom voom!* Devil Woman starts the car and edges towards the Leap of Death.

I look at her, horrified.

'Can you drive this thing?' I ask.

'I'm a stuntwoman,' she says viciously.
'I can drive any car.'

'Yes,' I say, 'but have you actually
driven this one over the Leap of Death?'

'No,' she says. 'But there's always a first
time!'

With that she edges the car over the cliff. I cannot believe this.

I can see Car Bonanza way beneath us. I can see crowds looking up at us. I can see crocodiles.

'*We don't even have a seatbelt,*' I tell her. 'You're about to drive us down a cliff!'

'Oh well,' she says, eyes madly gleaming, 'you'd better brace yourself.'

I brace my arms on the dashboard. Cat's arms squeeze round my waist. Devil Woman edges forward.

The front of the car is gently waving out in space, then suddenly . . .

. . . we PLUNGE
down the cliff.

I see the bottom of the cliff rise up fast, ready to *smash* us.

I am not even wearing a seatbelt! We are falling like a brick ready to go SMACK! But then, suddenly . . .

. . . we are HITTING the bottom of the CLIFF, our front wheels are SMASHING the curved road, and the G-FORCE HITS us. Cat is grabbing me, and the car *swerves* round . . .

The next moment, we are *accelerating* at eighty miles an hour towards the ramp . . .

Next we are *hitting* the ramp . . .

Then we are *MID-AIR*, and I have just
enough time to think: *Oh my God, we are
flying . . .*

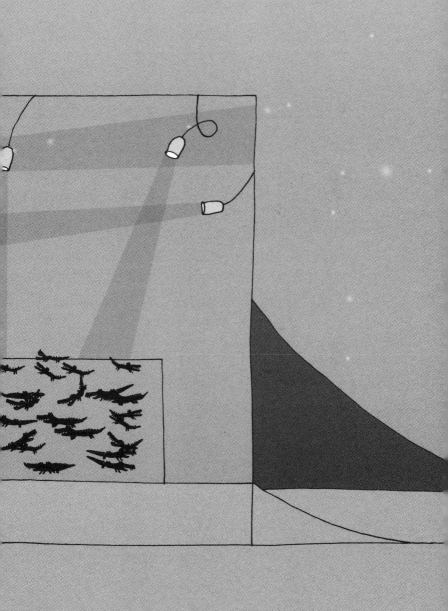

. . . over a hundred crocodiles! I can *feel* them out there.

I'll have the dog.

202

Then I think:

But there are two kids, one woman and a dog in this car . . . Are we too heavy to make it across?

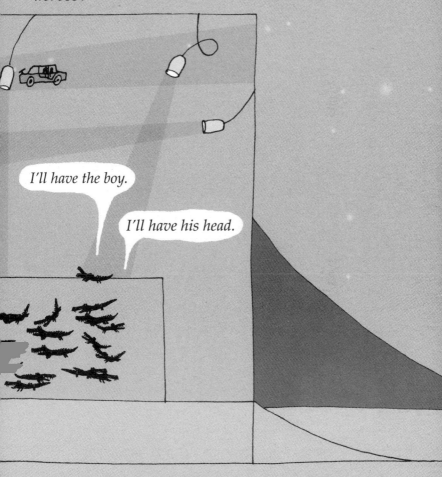

I see someone way down below me.

I'm thinking:

Is he about to see us DIE?

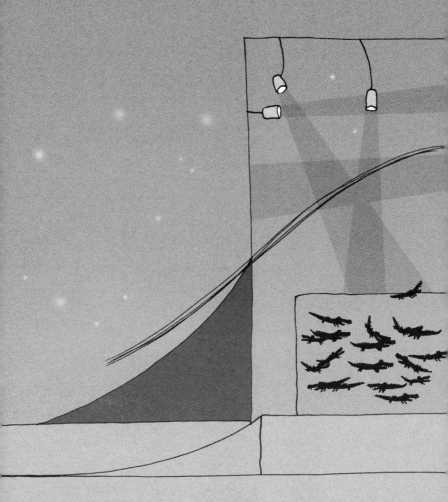

I'm thinking: *If I die, I'll never find Dad!*
When . . .

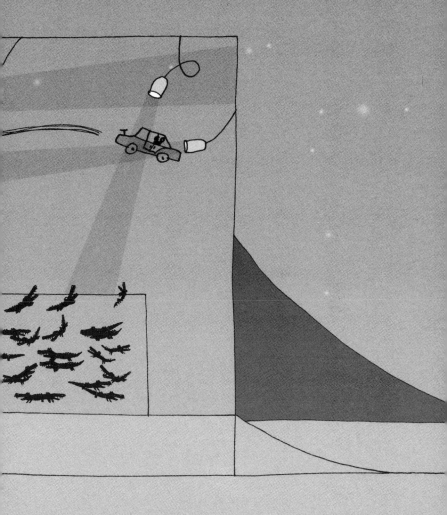

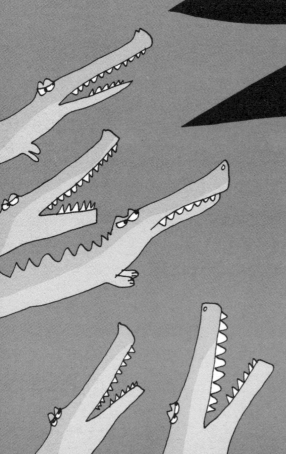

The car hits the other side of
the ramp and zooms off.

Cat looks at Devil Woman.

'You knew you could do that, right?'

'I didn't,' she says. 'I just figured it was the best option.'

'But,' I ask her, 'why are you running?'

She doesn't even answer. She just floors it.

As she comes off the end of the ramp and hits the field, she's doing sixty.

People are diving out of the way.

She now swerves out of a gate and up a country road.

She's doing seventy on roads meant for tractors!

'WHERE ARE YOU EVEN GOING?' I ask her.

As she reaches a big-hedged corner she's doing eighty. And we now see a huge crowd that CAN'T MOVE OUT OF THE WAY.

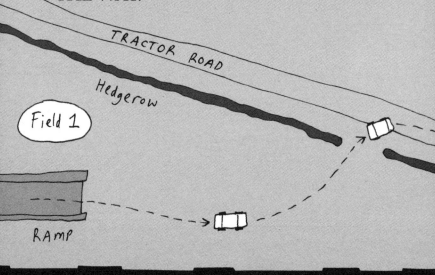

TRACTOR ROAD

Hedgerow

Field 1

RAMP

BALL OF DEATH

Devil Woman can't stop. Instead she . . .

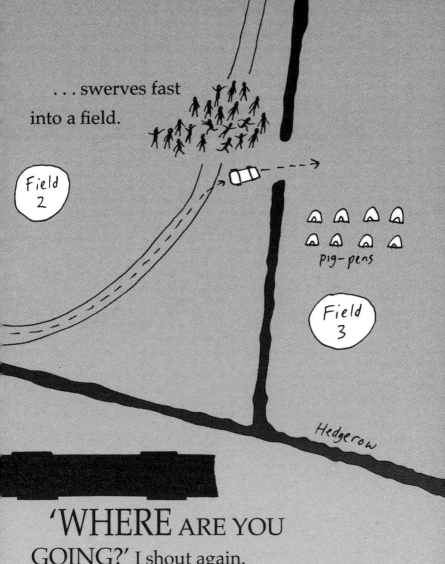

. . . swerves fast into a field.

Field 2

pig-pens

Field 3

Hedgerow

'WHERE ARE YOU GOING?' I shout again.

She doesn't answer.

She speeds through a gate, and it's suddenly clear where she's going . . .

CHAPTER ELEVEN:
Into the Sky

We're in the field for the World's Highest Ever Jump (done without a parachute). She's heading towards the plane.

I can see that the back door is open. I can also see the pilot, who is thirty metres away, sitting on a deckchair.

As we zoom towards him he seems to guess what we're up to. He jumps up and sprints through the opened back door of the plane.

Skidding in, Devil Woman leaps out of the car. She springs up into the back of the plane. The pilot tries to stop her. But she grabs hold of a fire extinguisher, and she LAMPS him.

Bang.

The pilot goes down.

We're now out of the car.

'Stop!' says Cat, but Devil Woman doesn't stop.

Cat now jumps aboard. Wilkins jumps up too.

So now there's just me. On that plane there is the suspect, Wilkins, and Cat . . . *What can I do?*

I jump up too.

For a moment I'm scared Devil Woman will lamp *us* with the fire extinguisher too. But she hardly even bothers with us. She's starting up the plane.

In five seconds the propellers are whirring and the plane is moving forward.

Ten seconds after that we're bouncing fast down the field.

I look out of the open back door. I can see fires and faces and dark hedges as we pick up speed. I see that we are in the very worst place for someone who is very, very scared of heights. *We are about to climb up into the sky!!*

Devil Woman pulls back the gear stick. The plane climbs fast.

Then she quickly puts on a parachute. *Why is she doing that?*

I see a parachute too. My hands are shaking terribly now, and I am so, so, so scared I cannot think, but I manage to put on the parachute, and I clip up all the straps.

Then I just sit. I don't know what to do. I can see Car Bonanza beneath us. I see bonfires. I see a stage with someone singing. I am *so* scared. I just shut my eyes, and I cuddle Wilkins.

I think everyone should have sausage dogs.

I think presidents should have sausage dogs, and when they are about to fire the nuclear bombs they should be forced to have a cuddle.

I think football managers should have sausage dogs. So then they wouldn't be swearing and shouting at the ref. They'd be cuddling the sausage dogs, who'd be giving them ideas.

I cuddle Wilkins. The murk in my mind clears, and I start to DETECT.

'*Why* did you put bleach in my uncle's car?' I ask Devil Woman.

She says nothing.

'I *know* you did it!' I tell her. 'I know you were friendly to us to give you an *alibi*. You *wanted* to be seen.'

She says nothing.

'But I still don't understand *why* you'd do it.'

'No,' she says. 'You *wouldn't*. Because you're a *Branagan* – the son of Padder Branagan – just as *Kenny* was his famous kid brother . . .'

She goes quiet. I need
to keep her talking.
  'So?' I say.

'I am *twice* the stunt performer he is,' she spits. 'I just drove over the Leap of Death with two kids and a dog. But that STUPID MAN gets the attention, because he is the *Branagan*!'

'So that's why you did it?' says Cat. 'You were *jealous*?'

'He's had his glory! It's MY time now!'

'*You tried to kill him!*' I shout.

'They're called stunts,' she says. 'If you're scared of getting hurt, don't get in the car!'

She has just confessed, right in front of us!

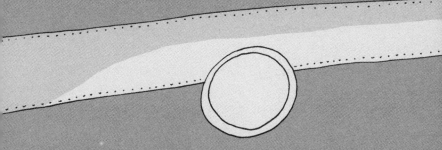

'WE WILL TAKE YOU TO *PRISON*!' I
shout. I don't know HOW I'm going to do
that, but I am standing now ready to DO
it. She is not keen to obey. Suddenly she
SMACKS me backwards, then
TURNS the plane.

I tumble back over the seat.

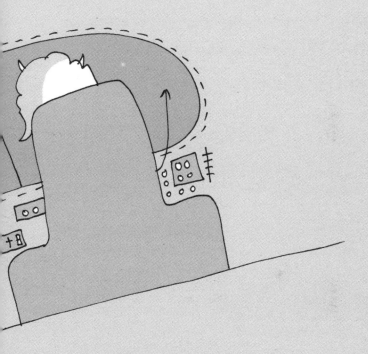

Oh my God.

The floor is very *skiddy* and the back door is *wide open* and the wind is *roaring* through it as if it wants to *grab* me. I'm sliding towards the door. I can't stop.

Cat holds me.

But Devil Woman is leaving the controls. She is stepping towards us.

'You shouldn't have made me tell you that!' she says. 'You shouldn't have got on this plane!'

And she lifts the fire extinguisher.

Wilkins LEAPS for her. He can't leap
higher than her leg, but he BITES that!
Devil Woman kicks him away.

'DON'T HURT THAT DOG!'
I shout.

'*I have had ENOUGH of you!*' she sneers.
She springs forward, ready to KICK me
out of the plane.

But Wilkins *trips* her.

And she falls out.

I can't believe it. Where Devil Woman was there's now just a big open door with the wind rushing through.

'But, *Cat,*' I say, 'who will fly the plane now?'

And I swear . . . *Cat actually smiles!*

(She's like this . . . When she's in the worst danger, she *smiles!*)

'I don't know,' she says. 'But *you* have a parachute!'

'But I don't even know how to use it!'

'You just fall and it opens!' says Cat. But then she adds, '*I think!*'

And those two words – 'I think!' – do not give me confidence. (Isn't there some CORD you're supposed to pull?)

'Here,' I say, 'why don't you have the parachute?'

I start to take it off.

'No!' she says. 'Keep it!'

I am *so* panicking!

'But, Cat,' I say, 'how the heck are we going to get out of this one?'

'I don't know,' she says, 'but I'd say this is the best option!'

'What?' I ask.

'This,' she says.
And she just pushes me out.

CHAPTER TWELVE:
Plunging Like a Brick to the Ground

From the very moment you are born your body knows one thing very well: *you should never, EVER find yourself falling to earth from a plane.*

I fall so fast my stomach *shoots out* of the top of my head, the wind *rips* at my cheeks, and I am so incredibly *TERRIFIED* I almost pass out.

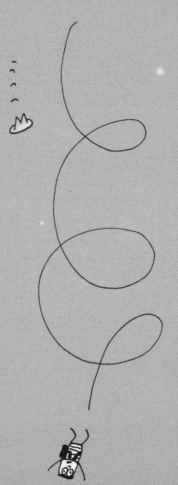

I am
spinning
down
through
space.

I can see the plane between my feet. It is
SHOOTING UPWARDS into the sky.

. . . As I watch it turns sharply in the air,
and then it DIVES down towards me . . .
and I see a tiny figure at the window. Even
though it is far away and tiny, I know who
it is . . .

It is Wilkins Welkin. For a moment he seems to be flying the plane.

He has his ears cocked, and you can just TELL he's thinking: *Don't worry, Rory, I am COMING for you!*

And I think: *Oh my God, I love that dog SO MUCH . . . Is this the last time I'll see him?*

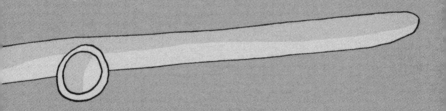

And then I think: *Did Cat just PUSH ME OUT OF THE PLANE?*

But THEN somehow the plane seems to
pull out of its dive.

I think: *Is Cat somehow FLYING
the plane? She seems to know how to do
EVERYTHING . . . but I don't think she can
fly a plane . . . CAN SHE?*

But I then
realise that there
is something
that is definitely
NOT flying . . . and
it's me . . . I am
looking down and
Car Bonanza is
RUSHING UP
FAR TOO FAST.

But THEN suddenly my parachute opens.

And then for a moment all the noise goes away. I look down. I can see the sea twinkling, and the mountains looming, and Car Bonanza beneath me.

If I wasn't so absolutely TERRIFIED
and WORRIED, I would probably be
thinking: *This is the most amazing sight I've
ever seen . . .*

I see a field. I see a bonfire. I see people
looking at me, holding up their phones.

Then I realise that I do have a parachute,
but that field is still approaching far, far
too fast.

I DON'T EVEN KNOW HOW TO LAND! That field is leaping up like a fist ready to smack me.

And then it DOES.

I hit the floor HARD. I am rolling. I am somersaulting. Then . . .

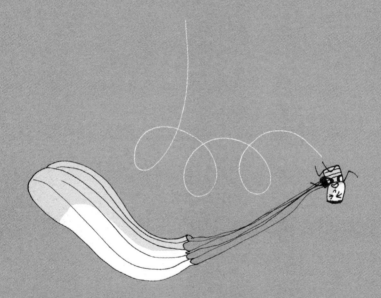

BANG.

CHAPTER THIRTEEN:
Dead

In my mind I am still seeing Wilkins in the plane.

Then in my mind I am seeing my dad on the day he ran off.

I realise my eyes have been shut for a while. I open them. I see stars. I see clouds. I hear a voice.

"oooooory!"

I sit up. There's a woman sitting right
by me.

"ooooorrrry!' she goes.

It's my mum.

My mum is an *emotional* woman. She does not believe in *holding herself back* at the best of times. Right now, she's just seen me falling from a plane, lying dead on the ground, then coming back to life. She does NOT hold herself back now.

'*Roooory!*' she *wails*. '*Are you OK?*'

'Mum,' I say, 'I'm *grand!*'

So then her mood changes.

'What the HECK were you doing,' she shouts, 'getting in that plane?'

And suddenly I see the problem.

'But, Mum,' I say. 'Cat and Wilkins are STILL in it!'

'What?' says Mum.

'Cassidy,' I tell her, 'my friend – she's on the plane!'

'Oh no,' says Mum. 'She landed a while ago!'

'WHAT?!!' I say.

None of this makes sense. A horrible thought hits me . . . *Am I actually dead*?

'You've been knocked out for a good few minutes,' says Mum. 'I thought you were dead!'

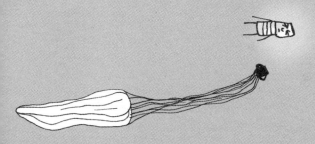

'But, Mum!' I say. 'What happened to Cassidy?'

'Oh, she's fine,' says Mum. She looks around. 'Look . . . here she comes now!'

I see Cat running towards me across the field in the blue moonlight.

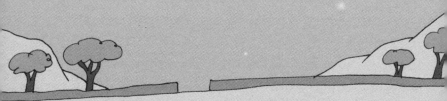

If I'm not dead, I think, is she a ghost?

But then Cat is panting before me.

'Cat,' I say, 'are you OK?'

'Oh,' she says, 'I'm *boomtastic*! I could fight a tiger, then eat it whole!'

'But I don't understand,' I say. 'You didn't have a parachute.'

'*No!*' she says proudly.

'So . . . HOW THE HECK DID YOU
GET OUT OF THAT?' I say. *'You can't fly a
plane!'*

'*No,*' she says, 'but the pilot *could*! I
woke him up. I got HIM to land it!'
'Oh! I'd forgotten about him!' I say.

'That's because *I'm* a better detective than you!' she says, and she dances like a cat wiggling its tail.

I *so* don't care about that now. There's something far, far more important . . .

'But, Cat,' I say, '*where* is Wilkins?'

And her face falls. And right away I just *know* the WORST has happened.

'Tell me what happened,' I say. 'Did he fall out?'

'Rory,' says Cat, 'he LEAPT out!'

'Did he?' I whimper. 'But *why*?'

'You know what he's like,' says Cat. 'He didn't know he was miles in the sky. He just knew you'd gone . . .

. . . so he followed!'

Oh God. I can imagine him falling!

I'm thinking:

Was he scared?

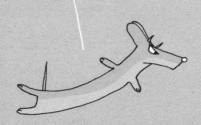

Then I am thinking: *Where did he LAND?*
We should find his body!

*We should give that dog the greatest funeral
any dog has ever had!*

Cat smiles.

'What?' I ask. 'Why are you smiling?'

'As you came down,' she says, 'didn't you hear the crowd over at the World's Highest Ever Jump (done without a parachute)?'

I don't know where this is going.

'What happened?' I say. 'Did they see the World's Highest Ever Jump (done without a parachute)?'

'We don't know,' she says, 'but it was definitely the World's Highest Ever Jump – *done by a DOG!*'

'What? Did Wilkins hit the trampoline?'

'*He did!*' says Cat.

Oh my God, I am thinking. I *wish* I had seen that! I can just *imagine* the crowd gathered to see the World's Highest Ever Jump.

Suddenly Wilkins shoots out of the sky like a METEOR!

EEEEEEEaaaaaaayuuuuuuummmm!!

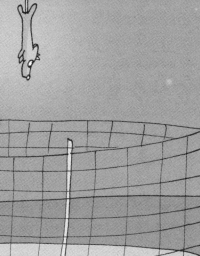

I wish I'd seen him as he HIT that trampoline, then bounced up HIGH.

I BET HE DID SOMERSAULTS!

I BET HE DID TRICKS!

'But, Cat,' I say, 'where is Wilkins now?'
'Oh,' she says, 'I think he's coming.'
Just then I see the world record holder
himself. He's with Mrs Welkin.

'WILKINS!' I shout.

He does his cocked-head look.

'WILKINS!'

He speeds towards me like a rocket. He hits me.

After that we are *hugging* and we are *sniffing* and he is *wagging* his tail, and for a moment I don't care about anything – *I have Wilkins!*

Soon Mrs Welkin is there too with the tiny train conductor.

'I wish Mr Welkin was here now,' says Mrs Welkin. 'He would be so proud. We just *stopped* another criminal!'

'The criminal was Devil Woman!' I tell her.

'I know *that*,' says Mrs Welkin. 'Her parachute landed right by the train. Michael Mulligan was shouting, "Stop that woman!" And I hear she took you, Cassidy and Wilkins in that plane!'

'Yes,' I say, 'but what *happened*?'

'We *chased* her down in the train,' says Mrs Welkin. 'Then I CLONKED her with the flask. Ooh . . . I hit her quite a few times! I had to be *pulled away by the police*!'

'Stephen Maysmith took her away,' says Mum.

For a moment, I imagine Stephen Maysmith taking Devil Woman away.

Then I think of my uncle.

'But is Kenny OK?' I ask Mum.

'Oh, he's a Branagan,' she answers. 'He'll live!'

For a moment I am very *glad* we're all OK. I am also very *shaken*. I could actually cry.

'Come on,' says Mum. 'Let's go and find your brother!'

CHAPTER FOURTEEN:
My Brother

As we approach my brother I realise that in the last hour *some* of us investigated a crime, drove over the Leap of Death, then LEAPT OUT OF A PLANE. But, *meanwhile,* my lanky EEJIT of a brother . . .

. . . *has not even moved!* He is sitting on the sofa with Julia. He is stock-still, just staring at her, like some *creepy waxwork*!

But then I realise he has made some *progress* in the last hour . . .

Julia is now holding his hand.

I would NOT want to touch that thing. It's always cold and *damp* like a squid that has died under a rock. But Julia doesn't seem to mind. They both look pleased.

Suddenly I want to get far, far away from this place.

'Who wants to get a drink?' says Mum.

I know if Mrs Welkin goes back near that train, we'll never get her off.

'Mrs Welkin,' I say, 'can we all just go home in the camper van?'

'Of course,' she says.

And that's what we do.

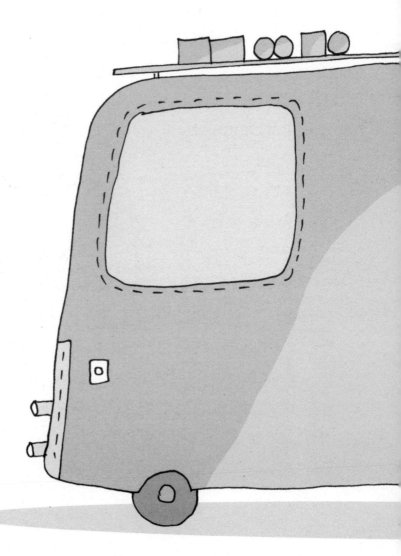

My brother sits on the back seat with
Julia. He's still holding her hand.

I don't care. I'm sitting in the front between Cat, Mum and Wilkins.

This is where I *am happiest*, I think – when I'm with them. Slowly I'm relaxing.

And so's Wilkins. He does a fart, but it's a tiny, gentle one – like a Frenchman playing his horn on a far-off mountain.

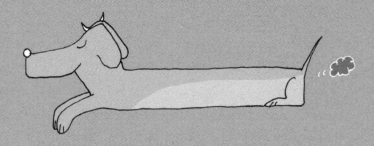

I am happy to smell it. I am *so* glad he's here! I'm so glad we *all* are!

As we drive off very slowly up the lane, I look out of the window. I see the moon, I see stars, I see a long *parade* of cars coming up behind us.

Ah, those cars can wait, I think. *Some of us in this camper van have just solved a crime. And others have just set a new world record . . .*

So I don't tell Mrs Welkin to hurry. I just look out the window. I enjoy the view. And I smile.

The End

About five minutes after I'd first met
Cassidy Callaghan, she found our first
clue about my dad – a picture of him by a
car.

But it takes months till it hits me . . .

'You know we saw a picture of my dad by a car?' I say to Cat.

'Yes,' she says.

'I have seen that car!'

'I don't believe you!' she says.

'It's on the way to school,' I tell her. 'I'll show you!'

And we don't mess about. We *run*.

Five minutes later, we are there.

We can see the car in a yard. Cat is smiling.

'What?'

'It's like they've been on a TV show,' she says, 'called *Make Your House Look Like a Criminal's*!'

'What makes this look criminal?' I ask.

'Erm,' she says, 'the reinforced walls with the six-foot barbed-wire fence. The security cameras. The signs saying "Beware of the Dog". All that leads to an impression.'

I look at the house.

A squirrel lands on the fence.

BANG.

It falls off.

I am not *so* sure I want to go in.

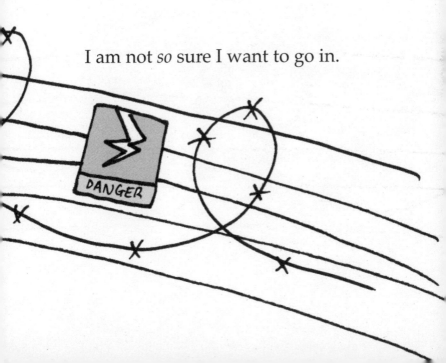

'If people buy cars off someone,' Cat says quietly, 'they *sometimes* leave paperwork in the glove box that would give the names and *addresses* of the *previous owners*.'

'You think my dad's address could be inside that glove box?' I ask.

'I'd say it's not *likely*,' she says. 'But it is *possible*. And as detectives we should ask ourselves: if we go in, *can something be learned*? And the answer, my friend, is YES.'

'All right,' I say. 'The only problems are the six-foot-high fence, the cameras and the dog.'

Cat gives me a *classic* Cat look.

I look into her eyes, and I think: *She's got a plan.*

Then I think: *But WHAT is it?*

To be continued…

Read more inside the next book!

Cracking the case wide open

RORY BRANAGAN
DETECTIVE
THE DEN OF DANGER

ANDREW **CLOVER** RALPH **LAZAR**

Coming soon!

Discover where Rory's adventures began . . .

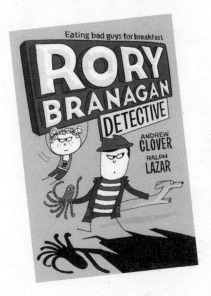

People always say: 'How do you become a detective?' and I say: 'Ahhh, you don't just suddenly find yourself *sneaking* up on baddies, or *chasing* them, or *fighting them*, or living a life of constant deadly danger – you have to WANT it. So why did *I* want it? I just wanted to find my dad.

And I will – but first I have to track down some POISONERS!

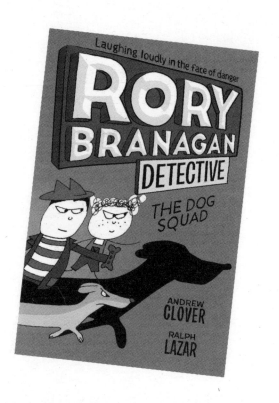

I, Rory Branagan, have uncovered a crime *right where I live*. Some *flip-flaps* are STEALING dogs. I am going to work out *who* they are and I am going to *stop* them, because I love *all* dogs. But the dog I love most, by about a *million miles*, is Wilkins Welkin, and he is in DANGER.

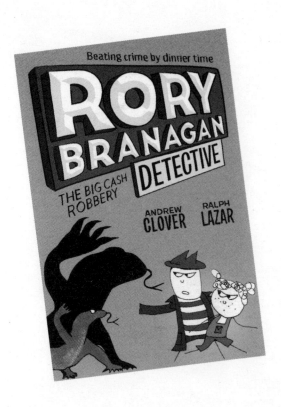

This week we had the biggest, *best* school fete
of all time. We had *bouncy castles, sumo wrestling*
and a real live *Komodo dragon*. We earned *loads* of
money, but then some evil *thief* stole it! So it's up
to me to find out *who* – and nobody will stop me,
not even a DRAGON!

My school is having a talent show – with Mr
Bolton's *ridiculous* rap, Mr Meeton's *epic* guitar
solos and my friend Cat's amazing dance – but,
right in the middle of it, there is the DEADLIEST
crime in the history of our school. I have to find
out *who* did it and *why* – before they strike again!